For Emily
—S.L-J.

For my little sparrow,
with love
—J.C.

Time to Say Goodnight

by

Sally Lloyd-Jones

illustrated by

Jane Chapman

HarperCollinsPublishers

Hopping bunnies, hop, hop, hop.
Stop your hopping, stop, stop, stop!
Stars are dancing in the skies,
Goodnight bunnies, close your eyes!

Little birdies, cheep, cheep, cheep.
No more songs now, sleep, sleep, sleep!
Night has come, and you must rest,
So climb inside your cozy nest.

Busy squirrels, one, two, three!
Time to curl up in your tree.
No more crunching, just be still!
Little squirrels on the hill.

Little owlies, what about you?
When night comes, what do you do?
Open your eyes! Leave your beds!
Lift your little owly heads.

Little bears in the dark wood,
Settle down now, as you should.
Stop that growling and behave,
Little bears in your dark cave.

Little fawn that's played and played,
When it's dark, don't be afraid.
You are safe now, we will keep
Careful watch, so go to sleep!

Tiny mouse, the day is done.
Stop your scurrying, little one.
No more squeaking, not one peep.
Close your eyes now, go to sleep!

What about
YOU,
sleepyhead?
Guess whose turn it is for bed!

No more dances, no more chat,
No more wanting this or that.
No more songs now, not one peep.
Close your eyes and go to sleep!

Stars are dancing in the skies.
Kiss goodnight
and close
your
eyes.

Time to Say Goodnight
Text copyright © 2006 by Sally Lloyd-Jones
Illustrations copyright © 2006 by Jane Chapman
Manufactured in China.

Library of Congress Cataloging-in-Publication Data
Jones, Sally Lloyd.
   Time to say goodnight / by Sally Lloyd-Jones ; illustrated by Jane Chapman.— 1st ed.
      p.   cm.
   Summary: In the same way that baby animals stop whatever they are doing and close
their eyes for the night, so a child must finally go to sleep when bedtime comes.
      ISBN 0-06-054328-0 – ISBN 0-06-054329-9 (lib. bdg.)
      [1. Bedtime—Fiction. 2. Animals—Fiction. 3. Stories in rhyme.] I. Chapman, Jane,
1970- ill. II. Title.
PZ8.3.J7538Tim 2006   2004030196
[E]—dc22

Typography by Martha Rago
1   2   3   4   5   6   7   8   9   10
❖
First Edition